AGASTYA

SAGE AGASTYA WAS KNOWN IN ALL THE THREE WORLDS FOR HIS WISDOM AND VIRTUE. ONE DAY HE CAME UPON A STRANGE SIGHT IN A FOREST.

WHO COULD THEY BE?

WE ARE YOUR ANCESTORS.

WHY ARE YOU HANGING HERE LIKE THIS?

BECAUSE YOU ARE NOT YET MARRIED. OUR SOULS WILL HAVE NO PEACE TILL WE ARE ASSURED OF THE CONTINUANCE OF OUR LINE.

AND SO DID AGASTYA CREATE A BEAUTIFUL BABY.

AT THAT TIME THE KING OF VIDARBHA WAS PERFORMING SEVERE PENANCES SO THAT HE MIGHT HAVE A CHILD.

THE CHILD, I HAVE CREATED, SHALL TAKE BIRTH AS THE DAUGHTER OF THIS KING.

A FEW MONTHS LATER THE QUEEN GAVE BIRTH TO A BABY. THE KING WAS OVERJOYED.

O BRAHMANS, MY PENANCES HAVE BEEN FRUITFUL. I HAVE BEEN BLESSED WITH A DAUGHTER.

THE BRAHMANS WERE IMPRESSED BY THE BEAUTY OF THE CHILD.

SHE SHALL BE CALLED LOPAMUDRA.

LOPAMUDRA GREW UP INTO A BEAUTIFUL AND VIRTUOUS GIRL.

I MUST FIND A WORTHY HUSBAND FOR HER.

MEANWHILE—

LOPAMUDRA MUST NOW BE READY FOR MARRIAGE. I SHALL GO TO HER FATHER AND ASK FOR HER HAND.

HE WENT TO THE KING.

I WISH TO MARRY AND BEGET A SON. WILL YOU GIVE ME YOUR DAUGHTER?

THE KING WAS TROUBLED.

HOW CAN I? BUT I DARE NOT DISPLEASE AGASTYA.

JUST THEN LOPAMUDRA CAME IN.

FATHER, WHY DO YOU HESITATE? I AM WILLING TO MARRY THE GREAT SAGE.

SO SHALL IT BE.

AGASTYA MARRIED LOPAMUDRA.

AFTER THE WEDDING –

LOPAMUDRA, YOUR ROYAL ROBES DO NOT BEFIT A SAGE'S WIFE. DISCARD THEM.

HENCEFORTH I SHALL WEAR ONLY BARK AND SKIN AND RAGS MY LORD.

LOPAMUDRA CAST OFF HER COSTLY ROBES.

COME, LOPAMUDRA. WE WILL GO TO MY HERMITAGE AT GANGOTRI.

BIDDING FAREWELL TO THE SAD PARENTS, AGASTYA LEFT VIDARBHA WITH HIS WIFE.

AT GANGOTRI, LOPAMUDRA HELPED AGASTYA IN HIS SEVERE PENANCES.

DEAR WIFE, YOU WILL SOON BECOME MY EQUAL.

THE DAYS PASSED AND LOPAMUDRA SERVED HER HUSBAND MOST EXCELLENTLY. ONE DAY—

LOPAMUDRA, YOU HAVE PLEASED ME WELL.

MY LORD, I TOO WISH TO BE PLEASED.

WHAT DO YOU DESIRE?

WE ARE HOUSEHOLDERS. IT IS CERTAINLY NOT WRONG FOR US TO POSSESS WEALTH.

LORD, I WOULD LIKE TO LIVE AS I DID IN MY FATHER'S HOUSE.

THEN I WILL GO OUT IN SEARCH OF WEALTH. WAIT HERE FOR ME.

AGASTYA SET OUT.

I WILL GO TO KING SRUTARVA. HE IS SAID TO BE VERY RICH.

WHEN HE REACHED THE COURT OF SRUTARVA —

O GREAT ONE, WHAT CAN I DO FOR YOU?

I HAVE COME TO YOU FOR WEALTH. GIVE ME WHAT YOU CAN SPARE.

SRUTARVA WAS A GENEROUS KING. BUT—

I HAVE NO WEALTH TO SPARE. HOWEVER, YOU MAY TAKE AS MUCH AS YOU WANT FROM WHAT I HAVE.

AGASTYA WAS WISE AND VIRTUOUS.

IF I TAKE ANYTHING FROM THIS KING I WILL BE DEPRIVING OTHERS.

HE TURNED TO SRUTARVA.

I CANNOT TAKE ANYTHING FROM YOU. LET US GO AND SEE IF KING BRIHADASTHA CAN HELP ME.

BUT KING BRIHADASTHA TOO HAD NO WEALTH TO SPARE.

PERHAPS KING TRASADASYU WOULD BE ABLE TO HELP. LET US ALL GO TO HIM.

HOWEVER WHEN THEY APPROACHED HIM—

MY REVENUE AND EXPENDITURE ARE EQUAL. BUT I SHALL COME TO YOUR AID IF YOU NEED IT.

NO. I DO NOT WANT TO ACQUIRE WEALTH BY DEPRIVING OTHERS.

THE THREE KINGS LOOKED AT ONE ANOTHER AND SPOKE AS ONE.

THERE IS AN ASURA CALLED ILVALA WHO HAS A GREAT DEAL OF WEALTH. LET US GO TO HIM.

ILVALA WAS A WICKED ASURA. HE HAD A BROTHER CALLED VATAPI. THEY HATED THE BRAHMANS AND HAD VOWED TO KILL AS MANY AS THEY COULD.

VATAPI, I HEAR THAT THE GREAT BRAHMAN SAGE, AGASTYA, IS COMING HERE TODAY. GET READY TO CHANGE YOUR FORM.

I'LL BECOME A GOAT AS USUAL. YOU WILL KILL AND COOK ME...

...AND FEED YOU TO THE BRAHMAN. THEN WHEN I CALL YOU...

...I'LL TEAR HIS STOMACH AND COME RUSHING OUT AND...

...ANOTHER HATED BRAHMAN, THE GREATEST OF THEM ALL, WILL BE DESTROYED.

WHEN AGASTYA AND THE THREE KINGS REACHED ILVALA'S KINGDOM, HE WAS READY TO RECEIVE THEM.

WELCOME, O SAGE, AND YOU, O KINGS. COME, I HAVE COOKED A SPECIAL MEAL IN YOUR HONOUR.

THE THREE KINGS WERE ALARMED.

ALAS! I NEVER THOUGHT HE WOULD DARE DO IT TO THE GREAT SAGE.

WE MUST WARN AGASTYA.

WHEN THEY TOLD AGASTYA—

DO NOT WORRY. I WILL BE SAFE.

COME, O GREAT ONE. EAT WITH RELISH.

AGASTYA BEGAN EATING.

HM..M.M! THE TASTIEST MEAL I HAVE EVER EATEN!

AND THE LAST, YOU HATED BRAHMAN.

11

WHEN AGASTYA HAD EATEN THE LAST MORSEL—

VATAPI, O VATAPI, COME OUT.

BUT—

BURRRRP

ILVALA BECAME FRANTIC.

VATAPI! O VATAPI! COME OUT. I, ILVALA, AM CALLING YOU.

HA! HA! HA! HA!

HOW CAN HE COME OUT? I HAVE ALREADY DIGESTED HIM.

ILVALA ACCEPTED HIS DEFEAT.

WHY HAVE YOU COME HERE? WHAT CAN I DO FOR YOU?

WE KNOW THAT YOU ARE WEALTHY.

THESE KINGS AND I NEED WEALTH. GIVE US WHAT YOU CAN WITHOUT DEPRIVING ANY OTHER.

ILVALA WAS QUIET FOR A MOMENT.

I SHALL GIVE THE KINGS 10,000 COWS EACH AND AS MANY GOLD COINS, TO AGASTYA – 20,000 COWS AND AS MANY GOLD COINS. I WILL ALSO GIVE HIM MY GOLDEN CHARIOT, AND HORSES.

13

THEN HE TURNED TO AGASTYA.

IF YOU CAN GUESS WHAT I INTEND TO GIVE YOU, THAT WILL BE YOURS.

AGASTYA WITH HIS SPIRITUAL INSIGHT EASILY KNEW WHAT ILVALA HAD IN MIND.

YOU INTEND TO GIVE THE KINGS 10,000 COWS EACH AND AS MANY GOLD COINS. AND TO ME, 20,000 COWS, AS MANY COINS, AND YOUR GOLDEN CHARIOT AND HORSES.

YOU HAVE WON THEM ALL. TAKE THEM.

AGASTYA AND THE KINGS MOUNTED THE CHARIOT.

I HAVE HEARD THAT ILVALA'S HORSES ARE THE MOST FLEET-FOOTED IN THE LAND.

THE KING WAS RIGHT. IN NO TIME, THEY REACHED AGASTYA'S HERMITAGE.

MAY WE RETURN TO OUR RESPECTIVE CITIES?

YES: OUR WORK IS OVER. YOU MAY GO.

WHEN THEY LEFT, AGASTYA WENT TO LOPAMUDRA.

I HAVE BROUGHT WHAT YOU WANTED, LOPAMUDRA. WE WILL NOW LIVE AS YOU WISH.

I AM GRATEFUL TO YOU, MY LORD.

A FEW YEARS LATER LOPAMUDRA HAD A SON.

AT LAST THE PROMISE I MADE TO MY ANCESTORS IS FULFILLED.

ONE DAY, WHILE AGASTYA, LOPAMUDRA AND THEIR SON WERE LIVING AT GANGOTRI...

...THE VINDHYA MOUNTAIN ADDRESSED THE SUN.

O GLORIOUS SUN, YOU GO AROUND MOUNT MERU EVERY DAY AND HONOUR HIM.

I TOO WOULD LIKE TO BE HONOURED IN THE SAME MANNER.

MY PATH HAS BEEN ASSIGNED TO ME SINCE CREATION. I DO NO SPECIAL HONOUR TO MERU.

THE SUN'S WORDS ANGERED THE MOUNTAIN.

THEN I SHALL GROW TALLER AND BLOCK YOUR PATH.

SO THE VINDHYA GREW AND GREW.

WHEN THE DEVAS SAW THIS THEY WERE ALARMED.

THIS UNCHECKED GROWTH OF VINDHYA WILL SOON PLUNGE THE EARTH IN DARKNESS.

LET US TRY TO STOP HIM.

THEY WENT TO THE RAPIDLY GROWING MOUNTAIN.

PLEASE DESIST FROM THIS PURSUIT. YOU WILL UPSET THE BALANCE OF CREATION.

THAT IS NOT MY CONCERN.

THE GODS DID NOT KNOW WHAT TO DO. AT LAST—

LET US HASTEN TO AGASTYA. HE IS THE ONLY ONE WHO CAN HELP US.

THE DEVAS WENT TO THE HERMITAGE OF THE SAGE.

WELCOME TO MY HERMITAGE, O DEVAS. WHAT CAN I DO FOR YOU?

O GREAT ONE, WE NEED YOUR HELP.

WHEN THEY HAD TOLD HIM EVERY-THING, AGASTYA REASSURED THEM.

DO NOT WORRY. I WILL DO ALL I CAN. GO IN PEACE.

THE GODS LEFT. AGASTYA TURNED TO LOPAMUDRA.

COME, DEAR ONE. LET US GO AND SEE IF WE CAN STOP HIM.

IT IS OUR DUTY, MY LORD.

THEY WENT TO THE MOUNTAIN.

O GREAT MOUNTAIN, I WISH TO CROSS OVER YOU TO THE SOUTHERN COUNTRY. WAIT TILL I RETURN.

O GREAT SAGE, I WILL STOP INCREASING MY SIZE TILL YOU RETURN FROM THE SOUTH.

SO AGASTYA WITH HIS WIFE AND SON SET OUT FOR THE SOUTH, CROSSING THE VINDHYA.

ONCE THEY HAD REACHED THE OTHER SIDE OF THE MOUNTAIN—

LOPAMUDRA, WE WILL NOT RETURN TO THE NORTH. THEN VINDHYA WILL NEVER BE ABLE TO GROW ANY TALLER.

SO AGASTYA AND HIS FAMILY SETTLED IN THE COUNTRY SOUTH OF THE VINDHYA MOUNTAIN.

THE KALKEYAS, A GROUP OF ASURAS, WERE BECOMING A NUISANCE TO THE THREE WORLDS. THE DEVAS WERE IN TROUBLE.

THE KALKEYAS ARE NOW ATTACKING OUR CITIES.

THEY DARE TO BECAUSE VRITRA LEADS THEM.

HE MUST BE DESTROYED.

LET US APPROACH BRAHMA FOR HELP.

SO THE DEVAS LED BY INDRA, THEIR KING, WENT TO BRAHMA. BRAHMA KNEW WHY THEY HAD COME.

GO TO THE GREAT SAGE DADHICHI AND ASK HIM FOR HIS BONES. TAKE THE BONES TO TWASHTRI AND ASK HIM TO MAKE A WEAPON FOR YOU WITH THEM.

WITH THAT WEAPON YOU, INDRA, WILL KILL VRITRA.

THE DEVAS GOT THE BONES FROM DADHICHI AND WENT TO TWASHTRI.

I WILL MAKE THE WEAPON VAJRA FOR YOU.

WHEN HE FINISHED HE TURNED TO INDRA.

TAKE THIS AND DESTROY THE ENEMY.

CONFIDENT OF VICTORY, INDRA AND THE DEVAS ATTACKED VRITRA AND THE KALKEYAS.

BUT BEFORE THEY COULD ADVANCE, THE KALKEYAS RUSHED AT THEM WITH THEIR MACES.

NOT EXPECTING THIS THE DEVAS BROKE THEIR RANKS...

...AND FLED IN PANIC.

INDRA LOST HEART.

WHAT SHALL I DO? IN SPITE OF BRAHMA'S PROMISE THE DEVAS HAVE DESERTED ME.

HE TURNED TO VISHNU FOR HELP.

DO NOT FEAR. I SHALL GIVE YOU A PORTION OF MY MIGHT.

WHEN VRITRA LEARNT OF THE HELP OBTAINED BY INDRA, HE ROARED IN ANGER.

COME, O LEADER OF THE DEVAS. TASTE OF MY MIGHT TOO!

INDRA WITH HIS NEWLY ACQUIRED STRENGTH HURLED THE VAJRA AT HIM.

THE VAJRA FOUND ITS MARK.

THE GREAT ASURA FELL DEAD.

WHEN THE DEVAS HEARD THE NEWS—

VRITRA IS DEAD. NOW WE CAN VANQUISH THE KALKEYAS.

THEY CHARGED AT THE HAPLESS ASURAS.

WE ARE DOOMED. THERE IS NO ONE TO LEAD US.

PANIC-STRICKEN, THE ASURAS FLED; AWAY FROM THE FIELD...

RUN! RUN!

...INTO THE DEEP OCEAN.

THEY WILL NOT FIND US HERE.

RID OF THE KALKEYAS THE DEVAS REJOICED.

WE MAY NOW LIVE IN PEACE.

MEANWHILE THE KALKEYAS ASSEMBLED IN THEIR UNDERWATER HOME AND PLANNED REVENGE.

WE MUST KILL ALL GOOD MEN ON EARTH. THEIR DEATH WILL DESTROY THE WHOLE UNIVERSE.

WE MUST DO OUR WORK BY NIGHT. WE WILL NOT BE FOUND OUT.

AND THE KALKEYAS BEGAN THEIR WORK OF DESTRUCTION.

E...E...AH!

WARRIORS AND HEROES WENT IN SEARCH OF THE MURDERERS, BUT COULD NOT FIND THEM.

WHO COULD THEY BE? WHERE DO THEY VANISH?

WHERE COULD THEY BE HIDING? WE HAVE SEARCHED EVERYWHERE.

INDRA AND THE DEVAS, WERE PERTURBED.

LET US GO TO VISHNU FOR HELP.

THEY WENT TO HIM.

LORD, YOU HAVE ALWAYS COME TO OUR AID WHEN WE NEEDED YOU.

WHAT IS IT NOW?

THE GOOD MEN ON EARTH ARE BEING DESTROYED.

WE DO NOT KNOW WHO THE CULPRITS ARE.

THE DESTRUCTION OF GOOD MEN WILL MEAN THE END OF HEAVEN ITSELF.

VISHNU TURNED TO INDRA.

WHEN VRITRA WAS KILLED BY YOU, THE KALKEYAS FLED INTO THE OCEAN BED TO SAVE THEIR LIVES. THEY ARE THE CULPRITS.

THEY CANNOT BE KILLED AS THEY HAVE TAKEN SHELTER UNDER THE SEA.

WHAT SHOULD WE DO?

WE WANT YOU TO DRINK THE OCEAN. THEN WE SHALL BE ABLE TO KILL OUR ENEMIES, THE EVIL KALKEYAS.

I SHALL DO WHAT YOU DESIRE AS IT WILL BENEFIT THE WORLD.

WHEN THEY REACHED THE OCEAN –

ARRAY YOURSELVES FOR WAR WHILE I DRINK THE OCEAN.

AND AGASTYA BEGAN DRINKING THE OCEAN.

AS THE OCEAN BED BECAME VISIBLE, THE KALKEYAS TAKEN BY SURPRISE RAN HELTER SKELTER.

WH... WHAT!

WHERE IS ALL THE WATER GOING?

RUN!

THE DEVAS WERE WELL PREPARED.

ATTACK! DO NOT SPARE A SINGLE ONE OF THEM.

A TERRIBLE BATTLE ENSUED.

BUT THE KALKEYAS WERE UNABLE TO WITHSTAND THE ONSLAUGHT...

...AND WERE SOON VANQUISHED.

AGASTYA WATCHED WITH HAPPINESS THE VICTORY OF THE DEVAS.

MY TASK IS ACCOMPLISHED. I MAY NOW GO BACK TO MY PENANCES. PEACE BE WITH YOU.

THUS ONCE MORE THE JUST AND WISE SON OF MITRA AND VARUNA SUPPRESSED EVIL AND PROTECTED THE GOOD.